"Look what I found!"

"TRACKS!"

TUMBLE grinned.
　　　"Let's follow them!"

TUM

A LITTLE BOOK ABOUT

BLE!

HAVING IT ALL

Written and Illustrated by MARIA VAN LIESHOUT

Designed by MOLLY LEACH

FEIWEL AND FRIENDS   NEW YORK

The three best friends

dashed down the hill.

They ran,
   ran,
      ran,

until . . .

That's when they saw the **red** thing.

"What is it?"

"Go touch it, TUMBLE!"

So TUMBLE *touched* it.

He *sniffed* it . . . .

. . . and *pushed* it.

Then, he quickly ran away.

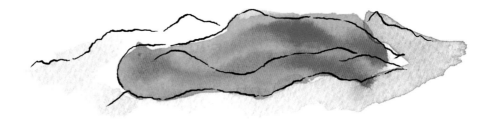

The red thing didn't move.

TUMBLE lifted it up.

It was soft. And warm.

"Can we touch it, too?"

"No!"

"It's mine!"

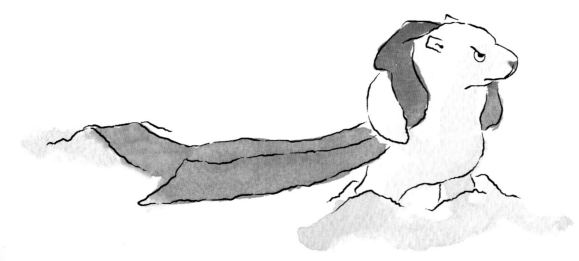

"Besides,
you don't know how to use this

. . . this . . .

. . . wubbie!"

SPLAT!

TUMBLE tripped.

"Can we help you
     carry the wubbie?"

"NO!" TUMBLE growled.

"I will carry MY wubbie!"

"We want to play with the wubbie, too!"

"OOF!"

"UMPF!"

MINE!"

Uh-oh.
TUMBLE was stuck.

"Can you give me a *PUSH?*
PULL?
PLEASE?"

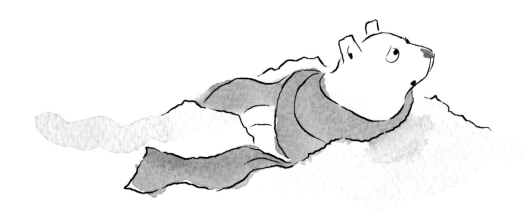

"Sorry, TUMBLE,"
   his friends said.
        "We can't touch the wubbie. . . ."

TUMBLE rocked and wobbled.

He jiggled and tossed.

"S I G H . . . ."

"OK, you can touch the wubbie,"

TUMBLE said.

TUMBLE's friends pulled the wubbie . . .

and TUMBLE . . .

up again.

"LOOK! More tracks!"
TUMBLE's friend called.

"They might lead to more **wubbies!**"

TUMBLE yawned and mumbled,

"I can't imagine a wubbie better than this one. . . ."

Voor mijn mam

A Feiwel and Friends Book
An Imprint of Macmillan

The artwork is created using pencil, ink, and watercolor. First, pencil sketches are traced with ink and scanned into the computer. Then the sketch is placed on a lightbox with watercolor paper so that watercolor may be applied; this watercolor layer is then scanned into the computer as a separate Photoshop layer. The ink line is traced with a writing tablet, and colored pencil is added where necessary.

Library of Congress Cataloging-in-Publication Data

Van Lieshout, Maria.
Tumble! : a little book about having it all / Maria van Lieshout. — 1st ed.
p. cm.
Summary: When three little bears find a red toy to play with and Tumble claims it for his own, this proves to be not such a good idea.
ISBN: 978-0-312-54859-9 (pob)
[1. Sharing—Fiction. 2. Bears—Fiction.] I. Title.
PZ7.V2753Tu 2010
[E]—dc22
2009050271

Feiwel and Friends logo designed by Filomena Tuosto

First Edition: 2010

www.feiwelandfriends.com

10 9 8 7 6 5 4 3 2 1